← To insure good luck, read thi

Madame Amelia

I see...
I see... It's getting clearer...
Yes! I see a bowling ball on a dog dish!

FIDO

Tells All

by Marissa Moss

(except fortunes and predictions by Amelia)

You could carry around a heavy horseshoe — or just use this book!

← fortune-telling fish
(lay the thin plastic in the palm of
your hand. If it stays flat, then
you're a cold fish!)

This notebook is dedicated to

Shelah –

I predict a sweet future –

you will eat many delicious fortune cookies!

If you copy
me, my crystal
ball will reveal
all!

Pleasant Company Publications
8400 Fairway Place
Middleton, Wisconsin 53562

Book Design by Amelia

First Pleasant Company Publications printing, 2001

An Amelia® Book

Manufactured in Singapore
American Girl® is a trademark
of Pleasant Company

I see in the future
many more printings!

These are not
lucky lottery
numbers —
don't play them! →

01 02 03 04 05 06 TWP 10 9 8 7 6 5 4 3 2 1

another kind
of fortune-telling
fish →

If you want
riches, bank on a
sand dollar!

I said to the
tuna, "You're all
wet!"

You'll
have a
whale of
a time!

I've always wanted to see into the future or read people's minds, but the closest I've come is dressing up as a fortune-teller for Halloween.

clip-on earrings

beads my mom brought back from New Orleans

plastic pumpkin for candy

puffy blouse I borrowed from Gigi, Cleo's best friend

I didn't see the future, but I did see a LOT of candy.

tablecloth becomes glamorous skirt

ballet slippers because tennis shoes just don't go with fortune-telling

Today at the carnival, I saw one of those mechanical fortune-tellers — the kind where you put in a coin and the dummy moves around until a little card comes out of the slot.

my card →

You know how to follow your ideas.
Madame Zitzka

That gave me the idea to make a fortune-telling notebook. I mean, I can do as good a job as a dummy! I definitely know how to read palms — I look at my own hands all the time.

fortune-telling → dummy

madame Zitska

money goes in here ←

card comes out here ←

Palm Reading

↑ a hands-on experience!

Hand it over! ↑

All those little lines and whorls on your hands are supposed to mean something, but I can read hands in a different way!

Hand with chocolate smudges ↙

↑ means this person just ate candy.

Hand with white dust sprinkled on it ↘

means this person baked cookies very recently. ↑

Hand with poison-oak
rash
↓

means this person went on
a hike and wasn't very
careful!

Hand that's cold
and clammy
↓

means this person was
holding an ice-cold can
of soda.

Hand with dirt under
the fingernails
↓

means this person has a
green thumb — or at least
a brown one!

Hand with a mitt
on it
↓

means this person wants
to catch a ball.

Hand with black
fingernail polish
↓

means this person wants
to make a strong fashion
statement (or be a witch
for Halloween).

Hand with ink
stains all over it
↓

means this person is
very creative, always
writing and drawing!

Foot Reading

Feet can tell you a lot about a person, too. You just have to know what to look for.

Foot with a very high arch

means this person wears high heels all the time.

Foot with curled-in toes

means this person needs to buy bigger shoes NOW! The old ones are much too small!

Foot with a toe ring

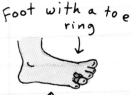

means this person doesn't mind snagged socks.

Foot with sand between the toes

means this person just went to the beach.

Foot that's very pale and soft

means this person doesn't go barefoot outside very much.

Foot with hairy toes

means this person turns into a werewolf during the full moon!

Foot that constantly jiggles

means it's hard for this person to sit still.

Foot with webbed toes

means this person swims like a duck!

Foot with long, sharp nails

means this person climbs trees barefoot and needs the nails for gripping (either that or the nail clippers got lost).

Foot with ink stains on it

means this person is very talented and can write and draw using only toes!

Footprints

mean this person stepped in wet paint and is tracking it all over the floor!

Quizzes can reveal as much about you as your hands and feet, so I'm putting a lot of quizzes in this notebook.

QUIZ #1
The Pajama Game!

Pick out the sleepwear you like best. Choose some slippers and a bathrobe to go with it. The combination you pick says a lot about who you are!

①

Ⓐ fuzzy, zip-up pajamas   Ⓑ flannel nightgown

Ⓒ oversized T-shirt   Ⓓ top and boxer shorts

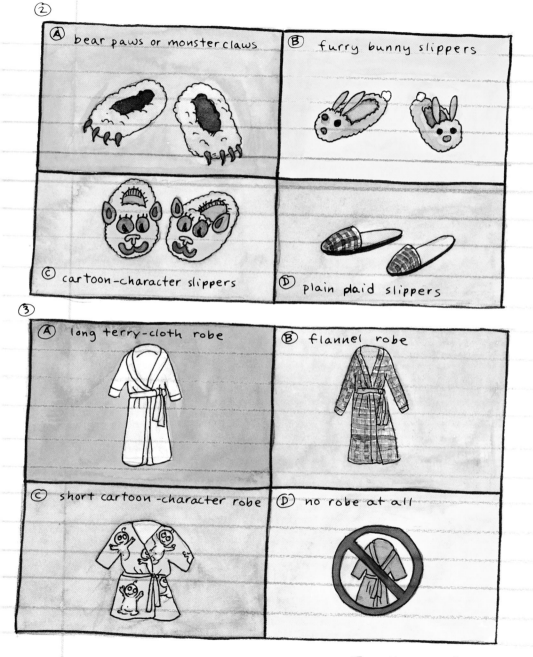

②
(A) bear paws or monster claws
(B) furry bunny slippers
(C) cartoon-character slippers
(D) plain plaid slippers

③
(A) long terry-cloth robe
(B) flannel robe
(C) short cartoon-character robe
(D) no robe at all

Turn the page for answers.

If you chose mostly A's, you like to be comfy-cozy
If you chose mostly B's, you like to be snuggly-wuggly.
If you chose mostly C's, you like to be cuddly-wuddly.
If you chose mostly D's, you like to be fuddy-duddy.

If you chose a mix of all the letters, you have a very distinctive style!

And if you're getting sleepy reading about pajamas, then it's time to go to bed.

Gggnnnaaak!

Cleo snoring in her favorite pajamas

cartoon-character T-shirt

big boxer shorts

furry monster feet

Bite into a Fortune

You can make your own fortunes or copy these. If you don't have fortune cookies to squeeze them into, put them in Oreos — but you'll have to lick off the cream filling to read them!

That's the way the cookie crumbles.

A cookie in the hand is worth two in the jar.

Dessert awaits those who eat their vegetables.

Put your cookie where your mouth is!

A cookie by any other name is just as sweet.

When the chips are down, eat them — they're chocolate!

When a Fig Newton goes stale, is it a Fig Oldton?

A cookie a day keeps the doctor away — but you'll see the dentist more!

Amelia's

Astrology is the belief that stars influence people. Astrological signs are based on constellations formed by stars — but anyone can find pictures in stars! (It's kind of like seeing things in clouds.) So I've made up my own constellations. Find your birth date and see what sign you were born under (or make up your own!).

Constellation
Banana Gigantus

↑
the symbol for Banana
(not to be confused with
a hot dog)

January 1 – February 15: Sign of the Banana. Sometimes you're slippery and make people fall, but other times you're a real treat to be around, especially for ice cream lovers. You get along best with Elephants.

I'm very
a-peel-ing!

↑
constellation
Earmufficus

↑
the symbol for
Earmuffs

February 16 – March 31: Sign of the Earmuffs. It's hard for you to hear what others have to say, but you know how to warm folks up. You like winter better than summer — you're definitely not a beach person. Instead you have a special talent for snowshoeing.

I'm all
ears!

I'm all
muff!

Astrology

Astronomy is the science of the stars — like how stars are born, what a black hole is, that kind of stuff. A black hole isn't a mud puddle. It's a very dense star — so dense that light can't escape its gravity.

← not the brightest star in the sky!

Constellation
Couchus
Potatocus
↓

April 1 – May 15: Sign of the Couch Potato.
It's hard for you to resist junk food, especially while watching TV. People look to you for answers to all kinds of trivia, since you've watched every game show at least 82 times. If you ever go on a quiz show, you'll win the jackpot!

the ↑
symbol for
Couch
Potato

I can read a book *and* watch TV at the same time!

May 16 – June 30: Sign of the QuikShop.
You're happiest when you're very busy. You hate being stuck in long, boring lines. Jumbo-sized drinks are important to you, but all food must be bite-sized or microwaveable. Friends — especially Couch Potatoes — know they can rely on you when they're in a hurry.

IN AND OUT!

Constellation
QuikShoppicus

Why drink a cup when you can hug two gallons at once?

GIANT GLUG

the symbol for
QuikShop ↑

Constellation
umbrellicus
↓

July 1 - August 15: Sign of the Umbrella.
During stormy times, you're a loyal friend —
some people won't go anywhere without you!
But a strong wind can make you change
direction and turn you inside out. To some, you're
all wet, but to others, you're a reliable partner.
You get along great with Earmuffs.

↑
the symbol
for Umbrella

Sometimes I
just get carried
awaaaay!

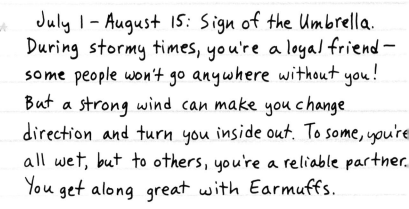

← Constellation Elephantus

August 16 - September 30: Sign of the Elephant.
You have a terrific memory and will work for
peanuts, so people love you — especially those born
under the sign of the Banana. You have a playful
side, too, and love water
fights.

Peanuts,
anyone?

↑ the symbol
for Elephant

October 1 – November 15: Sign of the Guitar.
Very popular at picnics and parties, you
have a busy social life. You're in tune
with others, so it's hard for you to
be alone. Pick a job where you're
surrounded by friends, and you'll be
happy!

the symbol
for Guitar

Hum a few notes,
and I'll follow
along.

November 16 – December 31: Sign of the Meat Loaf.
Some people find you comforting and warm. Mashed
potatoes bring out your best qualities. Canned
green beans bring out your worst (avoiding them is
advisable). But no matter what, you're solid and
dependable.

the symbol
for Meat Loaf
(or a brick, which is
what your stomach feels like
after you eat the meat loaf!)

Who'd have
thunk it?

A loaf of
meat?

Quiz #2
Are You a Carly or a Cleo?
(Or a Nadia or an Amelia?)

How would you react in these everyday situations?
Choose one answer for each question.

① You're washing dishes and you break a dish. You:

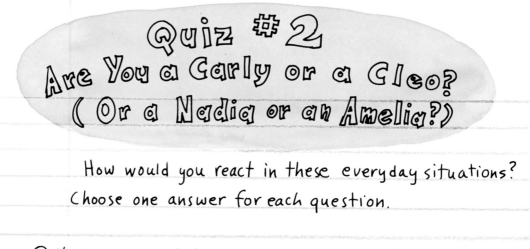

Ⓐ throw the dish away and then tell your mom.

Ⓑ tell your mom and ask her to throw away the broken pieces.

Ⓒ tell your mom an alien's face in the window startled you and made you drop the dish.

Ⓓ blame it on your little sister.

② You have a big test tomorrow. You:

Ⓐ study and go to bed early.

Ⓑ study and wake up early to study some more.

Ⓒ stay up late studying because you have to finish the chapter.

Ⓓ glance at your books and notes, but don't worry about it much.

③ Your mom tells you to clean out the refrigerator, a job you really hate. You:

Ⓐ do it as soon as you can to get it over with.
Ⓑ do it after you've finished the things you wanted to do.
Ⓒ offer to do a different chore instead.
Ⓓ clean out the fridge by eating all the food inside.

④ You bite into something that tastes extra delicious. You:

Ⓐ eat the way you normally do, but with a smile.
Ⓑ eat slooooowly and relish every bite.
Ⓒ hum a happy tummy song to yourself.
Ⓓ shove as much of it into your mouth as you can.

⑤ You're in the middle of a very exciting book. You:

Ⓐ read only when you have time to finish a big chunk.
Ⓑ read only a chapter a day so the book will last longer.
Ⓒ keep reading until you finish, no matter what.
Ⓓ get so excited, you read aloud to whoever's around you.

⑥ You get into a fight with your friend, and you're really mad. You:

ⓐ calm down before you talk to your friend again.

ⓑ try to see the other person's point of view.

ⓒ draw a picture to make yourself feel better.

ⓓ yell insults as loud as you can.

If you chose mostly A's, you know what you want and are practical about getting it.

You're a Carly!

If you chose mostly B's, you're a considerate person others can depend on.

You're a Nadia!

If you chose mostly C's, you know what that means! (The face on the right is a clue.)

You're an Amelia!

If you chose mostly D's, what are you doing reading my notebook?!

You're a Cleo!

Words of Wisdom

Some everyday sayings don't make much sense to me, so I've changed them to really be wise.

FIND YOUR SECRET SPIRIT NAME

   Sometimes I wonder what name I would choose for myself if I weren't named Amelia. I'd pick a name that described my spirit or personality, the way my camp counselor did. She called herself Rainbow (but her real name was Jane).
   To discover your own spirit name, find the word next to your birth date. Then find the word next to your birth month. Put the words together into one name (like the first of January = Bright Mountain). There you have it — the true you!

Birth Date:

1 – Bright	9 – Lightning
2 – Thunder	10 – Silver
3 – Sweet	11 – Raining
4 – Proud	12 – Soaring
5 – Big	13 – Rainbow
6 – White	14 – Dark
7 – Shining	15 – Blazing
8 – Leaping	16 – Glittering

17-Dreaming   24-Howling

18-Twinkly   25-Young

19-Whispering   26-Golden

20-Old   27-Fluttering

21-Diving   28-Cloud

22-Stone   29-Singing

23-Burning   30-Icy

     31-Feather

I'm Thunder Wolf!

Birth Month:

January – Mountain	July – Wind
February – Star	August – Fire
March – Waters	September – River
April – Wolf	October – Moon
May – Eagle	November – Tree
June – Fairy	December – Owl

I'm Proud River!

CAREER FINDER

Wondering what you'll be when you grow up? Well, wonder no more! You can tell your future by your birth date, the same way you found your spirit name. First go to the word by the day of the week you were born. For the second word, go to the date of the month, and for the last word, go to the month itself. Put them together to see what you'll be!

Day of the Week You Were Born:

Monday – Speedy   Friday – Crazy

Tuesday – Dazzling   Saturday – Amazing

Wednesday – World-Famous   Sunday – Bouncy

Thursday – Merry   Don't know – Powerful

Date of the Month You Were Born:

1 – Ceiling   7 – Celery   13 – Race Car

2 – Muffin   8 – Movie   14 – Piano

3 – Rocket   9 – Potion   15 – Storm

4 – Porcupine   10 – Magic   16 – Daisy

5 – Bathtub   11 – Elephant   17 – Dragon

6 – Cartoon   12 – Shadow   18 – Jewel

19 - Thumbtack   23 - Poetry   27 - Formula

20 - Fireworks   24 - Volcano   28 - Alien

21 - Robot   25 - Machine   29 - Airplane

22 - Balloon   26 - Pumpkin   30 - Seaweed

31 - Popsicle

Month You Were Born:

January - Blaster   July - Singer

February - Artist   August - Farmer

March - Inventor   September - Worker

April - Scientist   October - Doctor

May - Maker   November - Dancer

June - Washer   December - Builder

Quiz #3
Read Your Room!

Some people read tea leaves to predict the future. I think you can learn a lot more by looking at your bedroom. Just answer the following questions.

① Under my bed are:

Ⓐ two slippers, neatly lined up.

Ⓑ board games and books, artistically arranged.

Ⓒ all the things I shoved under there when I had to clean my room.

② In the closet are:

Ⓐ clothes, hung up in an orderly fashion.

Ⓑ clothes and toys, kind of organized.

Ⓒ I'm not sure what's in there — you could find anything!

If you think cleaning your room is hard work, think of the poor queen honeybee.

I'm pooped!

She lays 2,000 eggs every day!

All I s is a c cup

③ On my desk are:

Ⓐ pens, pencils, a lamp, and plenty of space to work.

Ⓑ papers, pens, tissues, a lamp, and boxes of paper clips, rubber bands, and thumbtacks.

Ⓒ I can't even see the top of my desk, there's so much stuff on it!

④ On my bed is:

Ⓐ my favorite stuffed animal.

Ⓑ a pile of stuffed animals.

Ⓒ a heap of all kinds of junk, including a stuffed animal or two.

⑤ On the walls is:

Ⓐ a bulletin board. Ⓑ a poster or two. Ⓒ such a spread of posters I'm not sure what color the walls are.

If you chose mostly A's, you're incredibly neat and organized. I predict you'll come clean my room.

If you chose mostly B's, your room is cozy and inviting. I predict you'll always be able to find what you need when you need it.

If you chose mostly C's, your room is a construction site. I predict only you will know how to get from the bed to the door without stubbing your toe on the stuff on the floor.

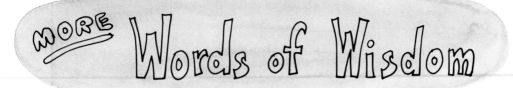

HANDWRITING

① How do you write?

Ⓐ straight up and down   Ⓒ slanted forward

Ⓑ slanted backward   Ⓓ every which wa

② How do you cross your t's?

Ⓐ in the middle: †   Ⓒ toward the bottom:

Ⓑ toward the top: †   Ⓓ next to the t: |−

③ How do you dot your i's?

Ⓐ with a dot: i   Ⓒ with a slash: ī

Ⓑ with a happy face: ☺   Ⓓ without the dot: ı

Oh, no, poor bald i! Don't forget the dot!

④ How do you make the tails of your g's?

Ⓐ slightly hooked: g   Ⓒ almost straight: g

Ⓑ very loopy: g   Ⓓ backward: g

g or q? Make up your mind! Is the tail wagging or what?

ANALYSIS

⑤ How do you make capital D's?

Ⓐ fat and jolly: D

Ⓒ dancing with energy: D

Ⓑ falling over backward: ◁
gravity-defying D!

Ⓓ skinny and hard to see: D

   If you answered mostly A's, you floss your teeth regularly, eat pizza with a knife and fork, and always look both ways before you cross the street. (Isn't it amazing what handwriting reveals?)

   If you answered mostly B's, you bend over backward to help people, never slurp your soup, and make your own valentines with lots of lace and ribbons.

   If you answered mostly C's, you squeeze the toothpaste tube from the middle, hold the school record for the long jump, and like to be the first one in your class to see new movies.

   If you answered mostly D's, you love to invent crazy things and eat odd combinations, like peanut butter and mustard, but have a tendency to forget why you started things. (Like why are you taking this test, anyway?)

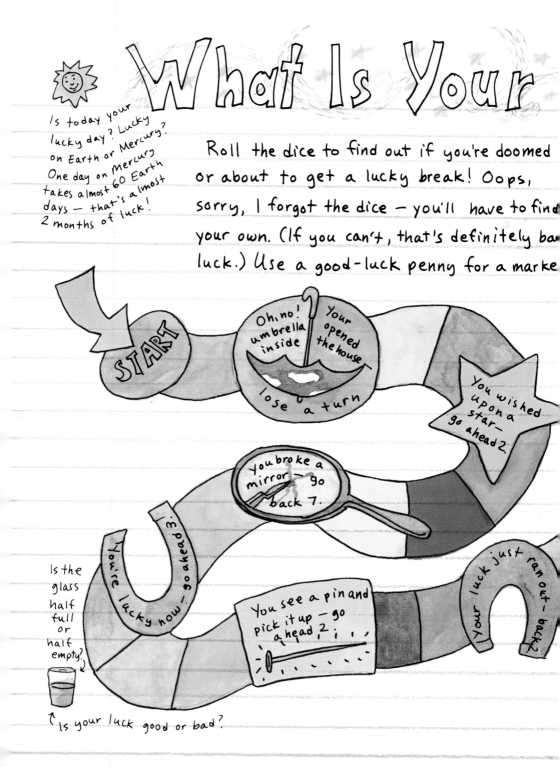

Your tastes in food reveal a LOT about your personality. Take this quiz to find out what your favorite snacks say about you.

① How do you like to eat vegetables?

② Which pickle would you pick?

③ Which flavor ice cream would you choose?

Ⓐ Rocky Road	Ⓑ mint chocolate chip	Ⓒ vanilla	Ⓓ butter brickle

④ What's your favorite pizza topping?

Ⓐ pepperoni and olives	Ⓑ pineapple	Ⓒ just cheese, please!	Ⓓ anchovies

⑤ Which chips do you dip?

Ⓐ tortilla chips	Ⓑ BBQ potato chips	Ⓒ plain potato chips	Ⓓ salt-and-vinegar flavored

⑥ What cheese do you chomp?

Ⓐ Swiss	Ⓑ cinnamon cream cheese	Ⓒ American	Ⓓ Brie
First I eat the holes, then I eat the rest!	Add jam to sweeten it up even more!	I love those individually wrapped slices!	The stinkier, the better!

puddle o'cheese

If you answered mostly A's, your favorite snack is crunchy to munch. You especially like food you can toss in the air and try to catch in your mouth.

If you answered mostly B's, your favorite meal would start with dessert, have a dessert main dish, and finish up with some nice rich chocolate.

If you answered mostly C's, you go for warm, comforting foods like mashed potatoes or macaroni and cheese. If you cozy up and eat snacks in bed, you're in heaven!

If you answered mostly D's, you like grown-up foods. Are you sure you're a kid?

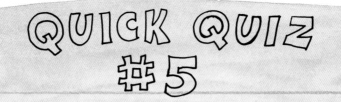

QUICK QUIZ #5

Penny Toss Test: Flip a Penny for the Answers!

a penny for your thoughts!

① Tomorrow you will...

Heads: meet a friendly alien and take a tour of its spaceship.

Tails: go back in time and ride a woolly mammoth.

Bring a coat — it's the Ice Age!

Whoa!

Welcome!

② When you grow up, you will...

Heads: own a candy factory and eat all the candy you want.

Tails: grow wings and be able to fly.

I love my job.

It's a bird, it's a plane, it's ME!

③ In your closet, there is really...

Heads: a secret passage to a hoard of treasure.

Tails: a drive-in movie theater.

gold and jewels

With popcorn, of course!

You don't believe these things are really true?

Isn't your penny full of common cents?

← Common <u>sense</u>, Common <u>cents</u> — get it?

DICTIONARY

It's good luck if:

there's a package waiting for you when you come home from school.

For me?

the math test is canceled.

Due to the fire drill, the test today is canceled. Sorry to disappoint you.

the ice cream store is out of every flavor but your favorite.

I don't mind a bit!

you drop your mom's favorite vase and it DOESN'T break.

Phew!!

your sister doesn't hear the bad name you called her.

What did you say?

Oh, nothing.

innocent look

your cup tips AFTER you've drunk all your milk.

So what?

no spill to clean up

✿ GOOD-LUCK SIGNS

You're a lucky duck if:

DICTIONARY

It's bad luck if:

# of BAD-LUCK SIGNS

You're an unlucky ducky if:

you drink the whole glass of milk and **then** notice the bug floating in it.

> Eww! Yucch!

you see something suspicious in the swimming pool.

> I don't want to know what it is!

> I'm just a frog.

your mom is too tired to cook.

> How about canned spaghetti?

> How about **not**.

your sister gets the last piece of pie.

> Deeelicious! One of Mom's best!

> Thanks for sharing.

you forget your brand-new jacket at school.

> Maybe it's in the Lost and Found.

> A brand-new jacket like that? I **don't** think so.

someone distracts you and makes you step in a mud puddle.

> Hey!

> What?

> oh, no!

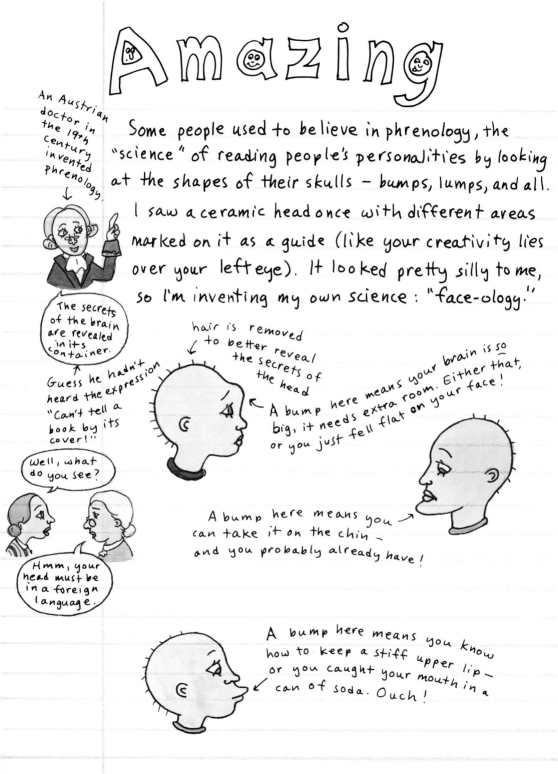

Face-ology

These kinds of bumps mean mosquitoes like to bite you. You must be extra delicious!

Get the calamine lotion!

Here's real face science— the average person sheds 40 pounds of skin by the time they're 70 years old! (Of course, that's from all over, not just the face.)

I'm losing face!

face particles

These kinds of bumps mean you may have chicken pox. Whatever you do, DON'T SCRATCH!

This kind of bump means a heavy object fell on your head. You need an ice pack!

Trick or treat!

This kind of bump means you're dressing up as a witch for Halloween. Better wear a hat though — there aren't many bald witches!

Spl✺tch✺l✺gy

For this test, look carefully at the splotches below and find the shapes of as many things as you can.

If you found mostly bugs, maybe that's because there are 10 quintillion insects alive in the world at any moment (not counting all the squashed ones!) — that's 1,000,000,000,000,000,000! Don't you feel itchy now?

HOW MANY DID YOU FIND?

If you found zero things, you may need glasses — better make an appointment with the eye doctor.

If you found 1-5 things, you know an octopus when you see one.

If you found 6-10 things, you have sharp eyes and a good imagination.

If you found more than 10 things, you're truly amazing! Nothing gets by you!

WHAT DID YOU FIND?

If you found mostly food, go get something to eat! You're too hungry to concentrate.

If you found mostly mountains and lakes, you're worried about your geography test. Better go study for it.

If you found mostly noses, you might need a tissue. Are you congested?

If you found mostly splotches, sometimes a splotch is just a splotch, but you never know... why don't you look again?

FROG POND

Ask the Pond a question, and toss a coin onto it for your answer. Try not to land in the water — it's too mucky for a clear response.

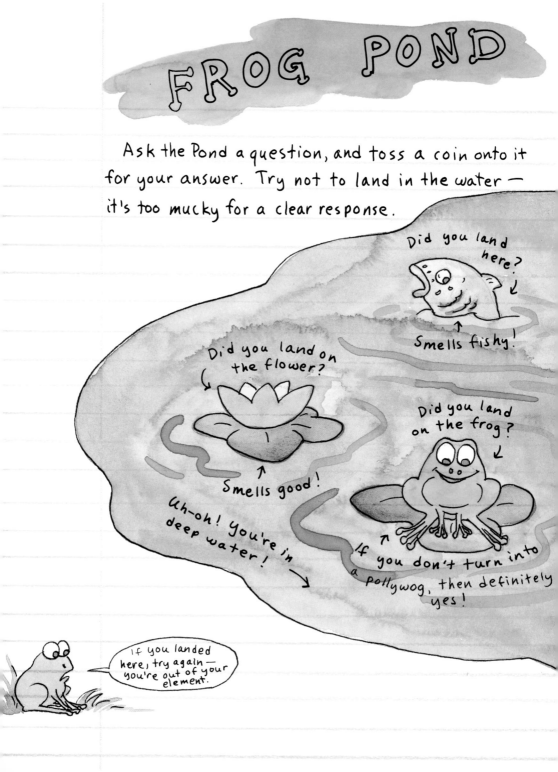

OF FATE

Did you land on a bug?
I'm not sure—a spider is blocking the answer.
You landed safely—all's well that ends well!
You're in over your head!
You're doing great! You caught a fly!
Did you land here?
Sorry, this frog has gone fishing.
Too weedy to say—try again.

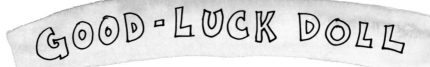

GOOD-LUCK DOLL

Cut out this paper doll of lucky positions. If you don't want to ruin your notebook, copy the page, then cut out the copy — or copy the positions with your body.

Cross your eyes for luck in seeing what's really important (but don't do it for too long or your eyes will stay that way).

Cross your fingers for all-purpose good luck (and protection from hangnails!).

Cross your arms (are you chilly?) for luck in reaching what you want. This also protects you from the bad luck of bumping your funny bone!

Cross your heart for luck with friends (and to ward off heartburn when you eat spicy food).

Cross your toes for no more blisters — lucky feet!

Cross your legs (do you have to go to the bathroom?) for luck in getting places. But don't walk this way!

A new kind of dance or a good-luck pose?

Wheel of Wealth

Wheel you have it or won't you?

Ask the wheel any yes-or-no question. Then toss a penny (preferably a lucky one) on the wheel to get your answer! It's easier to use than tarot cards and just as reliable!

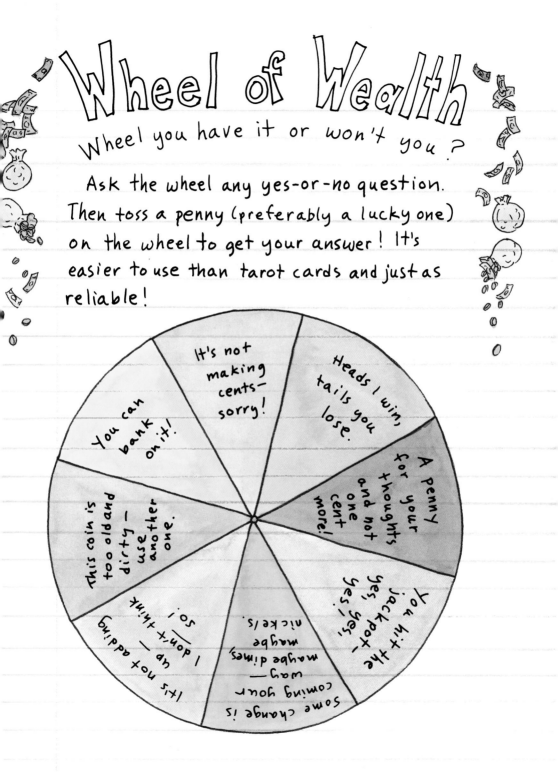

It's not making cents— sorry!

Heads I win, tails you lose.

A penny for your thoughts and not one cent more!

You hit the jackpot— yes, yes, yes!

Some change is coming your way— maybe dimes, maybe nickels.

It's not adding up — I don't think so!

This coin is too old and dirty — use another one.

You can bank on it!

QUIZ #6
WHAT YOUR SCIENCE FAIR PROJECT REVEALS ABOUT YOU!

You think it's just a school assignment, but actually your science fair project is a window into the secret workings of your brain. Take this test to find out about the real you.

How to change a boring object into 3 cool science fair projects:

① You prefer projects about:

ordinary parking meter

1. Do parking meters give you your money's worth? Observe and measure how accurate several meters are.

2. How does a meter know how much money you put in it?

It's me!

Build a model that shows how it's done.

3. Invent a new and improved parking meter.

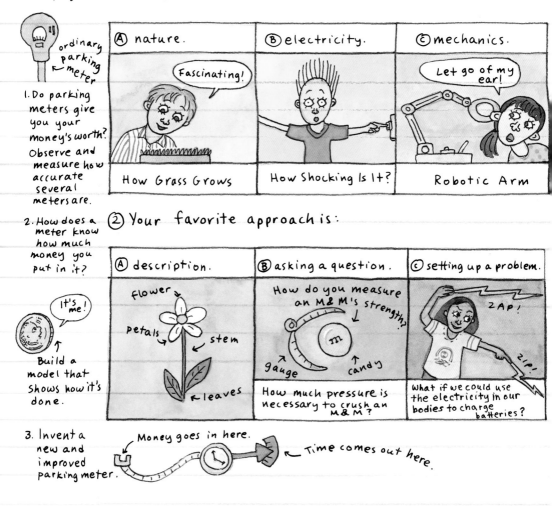

Ⓐ nature. — Fascinating! — How Grass Grows

Ⓑ electricity. — How Shocking Is It?

Ⓒ mechanics. — Let go of my ear! — Robotic Arm

② Your favorite approach is:

Ⓐ description. — flower, petals, stem, leaves

Ⓑ asking a question. — How do you measure an M&M's strength? gauge candy m — How much pressure is necessary to crush an M&M?

Ⓒ setting up a problem. — ZAP! zip! — What if we could use the electricity in our bodies to charge batteries?

Money goes in here. — Time comes out here.

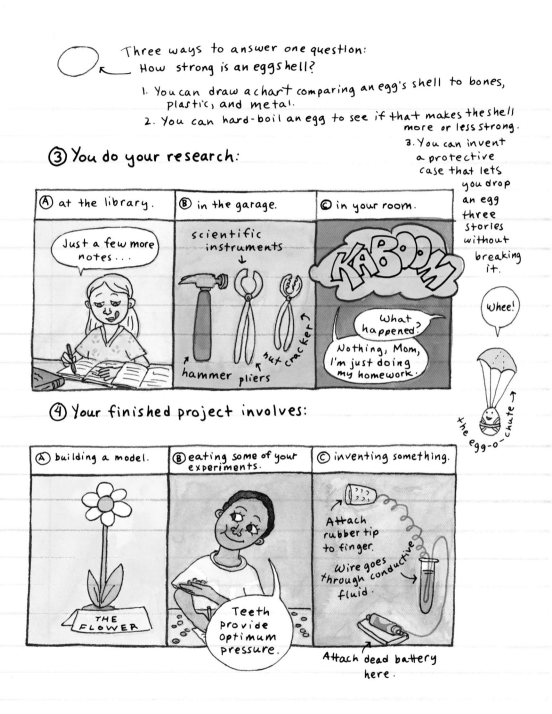

⑤ You like results that:

Ⓐ confirm what you thought.

"I knew it!"

Ⓑ are the opposite of what you expected.

"Who would have thought M&M's could be so tough?"

"I had to eat 63 bags to get my results, but it was worth it!"

Ⓒ completely surprise you.

"I can't believe it works!"

BZzZ

If you answered mostly A's, you're very curious about the world, a lot like physicist Marie Curie, the first woman to win the Nobel prize. She won twice — once in chemistry and once in physics!

If you answered mostly B's, you like to tinker around and figure out how things work, a lot like Thomas Edison, the inventor of the lightbulb.

If you answered mostly C's, you don't mind taking chances, even if you're often wrong. For you it's fun just to see what will happen, a lot like Rube Goldberg. He was a cartoonist who drew funny, complicated devices for simple tasks.

"I'll make a lemon-seed extractor! I'll need 62 gears, a crank, a banana peel, 2 balloons, a lever, 8 rubber bands, and a Ping-Pong ball."

ONCE AGAIN THE CRYSTAL BALL REVEALS ALL!

You get a second chance! Ask a yes-or-no question, then turn the page quickly for the answer.

Your Future Is In <u>YOUR</u> Hands!

This notebook gives you lots of ways to predict the future and understand the present. But if you want to make your future great — I mean make things happen the way <u>you</u> want them to — you need to take fate into your own hands.

Madame Amelia's Fortune-tellers

I designed my own fortune-tellers to play with. Some people call them "cootie catchers." Whatever you call them, I think they're great (even if they don't really predict the future)!

To fold a fortune-teller:

1. Carefully tear out a fortune-teller and place it picture-side down

2. Fold each corner into the center of the square, creasing the edges tightly. The numbers should be in the center.

3. Flip the fortune-teller over. Fold each corner into the center of this smaller square.

4. Fold in half horizontally and crease.

5. Fold in half vertically and crease.

6. Put your index fingers and thumbs into the flaps — you're ready

To use a fortune-teller:

1. Choose a number from the outside of the fortune-teller. Open and close your fingers that number of times.

2. Choose a picture from inside the fortune-teller. Spell out that word, opening or closing your fingers for each letter.

3. Repeat step 2.

4. Pick one more picture from inside and open that flap — it's your fortune!

Who invented fortune-tellers anyway?

I wonder about things like that.

You can play with a fortune-teller by yourself, but it's more fun with a friend